AF406746

BENEATH THE SURFACE
OF APPEARANCES

J. F. Rhodehouse

BENEATH THE SURFACE OF APPEARANCES

When evil lurks among us

EDITORIAL
LETRA MINÚSCULA

To Montse, my source of support and for her
patience with me.

To Gloria, my mother, for helping me with the
publication of this book.

To our cat Tai, for keeping me company
during the late-night writing hours.

Attention:

This book is not recommended for children
under the age of 16.

Index

AUTHOR'S PROLOGUE

For many years, publishing a book lingered like a deferred dream. "Beneath the Surface of Appearances: When Evil Lurks Among Us" is a short novel of mystery and urban contemporary fantasy genres.

This novella signifies my initial foray into fiction writing, distancing myself from other more informative pieces I have penned and the culmination of that yearning to write a book.

Publishing a book is an arduous undertaking that demands time and resources. From the initial writing and its revisions to the formatting and graphic design, each stage has been a step toward realizing a long-awaited dream.

Your decision to explore this tale is a vote of confidence that I greatly appreciate. If, after reading the following pages, you find a good experience within them, I invite you to share your opinion through a review on Amazon or other platforms.

Your words will encourage me and catalyze the creation of future, even more ambitious stories. No one is born fully versed, and the art of writing is a long path of continuous learning.

I sincerely hope you enjoy the story you are about to embark upon.

J. F. RHODEHOUSE

Evil is an illusion, a shadow of reality.

Celtic Wisdom

CHAPTER 1

THE "ORANGE BUDDHA"

The apartment was a blank canvas, a future ready to be painted by the hands of George and Montana. From the tranquility of their balcony to the spacious terrace that promised moments of relaxation and fun, every nook and cranny seemed to hide stories waiting to be discovered. It promised them a new life, a place where their dreams and secrets would take shape, and their refuge. However, a figure lurked in the shadows, challenging the privacy they so craved.

After months of searching, they finally found the perfect apartment: a duplex in a quiet residential neighborhood. Situated on the third floor, it boasted a balcony on the lower level and a spacious terrace above. Both spaces enjoyed a privileged south-facing orientation, providing beautiful views of the neighboring buildings" backyards. From the terrace, one could relish an impressive panoramic view of the cereal fields and the mountains with their pine forests. A painting of green and yellow strokes beneath a canvas of blue sky.

The place was perfect for their precious orange cat, aptly named Sunny. He quickly adapted to his new home. In particular, he adored the top part of the duplex, where he could bask in the sunlight filtering through the window panes and venture out to the terrace, exploring the neighboring roofs with feline curiosity.

But a man in his sixties resided just behind a rather aged block of flats across the inner courtyards of the cluster of buildings, approximately one hundred feet away. He was of short stature, with a round face, sparse hair, and a noticeable paunch. Perched on his nose were small round glasses that magnified his penetrating gaze. His attire almost always consisted of an orange T-shirt, as if his entire wardrobe was limited to that singular piece, or perhaps he possessed a whole collection of T-shirts in the same hue. With a touch of irony, Montana promptly dubbed him the "Orange Buddha."

That enigmatic neighbor would occasionally go out to smoke on his terrace. At those times, they could see how his dark eyes behind those glasses would gaze brazenly at their apartment, piercing through the glass panes of the balcony window that opened onto her balcony without shame. From his privileged position, he could observe their cozy dining room and the elegant wooden and steel staircase that rose from there to the upper part of the duplex. The rest of the apartment remained hidden from that curious and defiant gaze simultaneously. However, he could also see the couple if they approached the southern edge of their terrace.

While enjoying dinner on the terrace on a warm summer night, the string of lights that George had installed emitted a warm and inviting light around them, creating an intimate and pleasant atmosphere. Montana tried to minimize the importance of her curious neighbor's peculiar behavior. Knowing that the orange neighbor was in his room with his terrace door open, perhaps writing or drawing in the faint orange light that illuminated the room, she spoke in a low voice, fearing that he could hear her from a distance. "George, he's probably just lonely and bored. Maybe he doesn't have much to do and entertains himself by watching others. Don't worry about him too much."

George nodded. "You're right, honey. Maybe he's just lacking some distraction in his life. But his constant stares make me feel like I'm being watched like he wants to scrutinize every detail of our intimacy when we're in the dining room."

Montana took his hand to comfort him. "Don't let that ruin our happiness in our new home, honey. Let's enjoy what we have and not allow a nosy neighbor to disturb our peace."

George nodded again, but not without showing his concern. "You're right, but sometimes I feel like his eyes are watching our routine, our conversations. And those drawings he hangs in his room near the door. What could they mean? What if they have something to do with us?"

Montana smiled and gently put her hand on his shoulder. "Come on, my love, you're letting your imagination run wild. It must be his hobby. He draws and then hangs what he likes the most there so he can contemplate it."

Although George wanted to accept Montana's comforting words, the feeling of being watched still lingered in his head. That mysterious man, the "Orange Buddha", as Montana had nicknamed him, had become an enigma to George. What intentions did that neighbor hide behind that piercing gaze, those round glasses, and the enigmatic drawings he hung near the door? What were they about? George's curiosity grew with each passing day; it had almost become an obsession to uncover the reason for his relentless scrutiny. Was it merely prying, or did he harbor malicious intent toward them?

The next day, George was home alone, immersed in his work in front of the computer. As a programmer, he had the advantage of doing his work from the comfort of his home when attending the office in person was unnecessary. From his desk, he heard the "Orange Buddha" coughing on his terrace. "What a nasty cough" he thought, "it looks like smoking is taking him the toll." He observed that the door to that neighbor's room remained ajar. At the same time, the enigmatic sheets of white paper he drew swayed capriciously at the mercy of the current of air.

George's curiosity once again consumed him. Being an amateur ornithologist, he possessed a pair of high-quality binoculars for observing birds. He decided to use them to get a glimpse of what the "Orange Buddha" was drawing and hanging near the exit of his terrace. Patiently, he waited for him to leave the room and move to another part of his apartment. Once he had the opportunity, he took the binoculars and focused them on the mysterious hanging papers.

However, the sheets of paper were not entirely facing his balcony; they seemed to be arranged towards the table the "Orange Buddha" occupied in his room. The inconvenient current of air made the situation even worse, making it difficult to see. As George held the binoculars, his perseverance paid off. He could make out a drawing that seemed curiously familiar in the dancing sheets of paper. On it, the figure of an orange cat seemed to be depicted, which reminded him of Sunny, his cat. And on the sheet just below, the drawing of a bird that appeared to be a magpie.

Just at that precise moment, when George was about to delve even deeper into contemplating other drawings, the neighbor entered. He suddenly appeared in his room and closed the white wooden door with square windows with determination. George was suddenly deprived of his vision of those enigmatic drawings.

George sighed resignedly and returned to the laptop, immersing himself again in his work. After a few hours, his beloved Montana arrived home. She worked in a clothing store in the city center. Her presence always radiated energy and vitality. Montana stood out for her height and attractiveness; her long, light brown hair framed her face elegantly. Her modern and sophisticated attire reflected confidence with every step she took. In contrast, George, slightly taller than her, had short dark brown hair and preferred a more classic and sober wardrobe. Despite their differences, they formed a couple that fit perfectly together, complementing each other in every aspect of their lives.

"Hi, honey!" Montana exclaimed, leaning down to give him a quick kiss on the lips. "How was your day?"

George looked up and smiled back at her. "It was a quiet day. I finally saw the "Orange Buddha's" drawings through the binoculars today."

Montana raised an eyebrow in curiosity. "And what did you see? Is that guy a good artist?"

George explained, "He seems to draw them with crayons or colored markers, or both. In one drawing, I saw an orange cat sitting, very similar to our Sunny, and on the other one, what looked like a magpie. You know it's a pretty unmistakable bird, with its black and white colors and long tail."

Montana sat down on the edge of the table, intrigued. "An orange cat and a magpie? That seems pretty peculiar."

George frowned slightly. "It's strange, isn't it, that he drew a cat so much like Sunny? He even had a black collar like his."

Montana thought for a moment. "It could just be a coincidence. Maybe he saw Sunny walking on the rooftops. Like the magpie, they also venture from the park next door."

George nodded, though his expression was still thoughtful. "Yeah, it's possible. The truth is, it doesn't matter. By the way, he's not a Rembrandt at drawing; he's more of an amateur."

Together, they went to the kitchen to prepare dinner and enjoy a peaceful night in their new home.

The next day, George spent his entire day out of the house, immersed in his work. When he returned home, he was met with an unusual scene. Montana was standing on the balcony with a worried expression, looking out at the backyards of the buildings. "What's wrong, honey?" George inquired as he put his suitcase with his laptop aside.

Montana turned to him with a concerned look. "I can't find Sunny. He was inside the house when I left, but now I don't see him anywhere."

George frowned, trying to remember. "Maybe you opened the sliding French window of the terrace to ventilate, and he went outside without you seeing him."

Montana's concern intensified. "Well, if he was outside all day, he could be lost, or something could have happened to him."

George approached her and hugged her gently. "Don't worry, honey. You know Sunny is an adventurer. Maybe he decided to explore a bit. You know him; he loves to roam the rooftops and snoop around. He's sure to be back soon."

Montana nodded, although she still looked worried. "I hope you're right. I'm just worried that something might have happened to him or if someone has hurt him. You know there are ruthless people."

George stroked her face tenderly. "Let's wait for him together, okay? We'll look for him if he takes too long to appear, especially if he misses his dinner time.

Montana smiled at him gratefully. "You're right, George. He always comes back. But until then, I won't be calm."

So, the couple stayed on the terrace, waiting for the return of their beloved cat while sharing some moments of mutual support.

After a while, a magpie suddenly appeared and perched on the stone that covered the brick wall at the southern edge of their terrace, just a few feet away. The surprise was enormous when they realized the bird was holding a black collar with sparkling Swarovski crystals in its beak, glittering under the soft light of dusk. It was their cat Sunny's collar! Suddenly, a brief caw, characteristic of magpies, broke the icy silence. George jumped up from his chair in a hurry, full of anxiety. Just at that moment, the corvid took flight, flying over the rooftops, heading west towards the park, bringing with it the collar of their beloved Sunny.

CHAPTER 2:

THE REVELATION

A new caw echoed in the distance, like an eerie echo of the strange scene they had just witnessed. Montana was visibly shaken, her gaze fixed where the magpie had perched. "Can you believe what we just saw? That magpie had Sunny's collar! How is that possible?"

George said, clearly upset. "It's too much of a coincidence, don't you think? One day after I saw that drawings in the "Orange Buddha's" room, Sunny disappears, and then a magpie appears wearing his collar."

Montana nervously bit her lip. "What does all this mean? Did that neighbor know that damn magpie would get Sunny's collar?"

George, a sense of powerlessness in his expression, replied. "I don't know, honey, but I find it too much of a coincidence. It could be that the "Orange Buddha" had something to do with Sunny's disappearance."

Montana looked at George, disbelief in her eyes, trying to find some rational explanation. "It could just be a coincidence, couldn't it? Perhaps the 'Orange Buddha' saw Sunny at some point and noticed a magpie in the park, which inspired him to create those drawings. I don't think it necessarily has anything to do with Sunny's disappearance. Besides, as you know, magpies are known for picking up shiny objects and taking them to their nests."

George sighed, pondering Montana's words. "Maybe you're right, my love. It could just be that, a coincidence. But it's still strange, isn't it? That neighbor is always there, watching from his room, from the terrace. And that drawings? It seems like too much of a coincidence to me. How can a magpie take possession of a cat's collar? How could it ever be removed from it? It's a bird, not a person. I'm afraid there's something dark behind all of this."

Still with concern reflected on her face, Montana decided to change the conversation's focus. "Let's stop speculating for a moment. The most important thing right now is to find Sunny. We can't just sit here and do nothing."

George nodded, sharing Montana's determination. "You're right, honey. We have to act. But where do we start?"

Montana looked around, thoughtful. "We should begin by asking our neighbors. It's possible that someone has seen Sunny or knows something about what happened. We could start with the neighbor on the other side of the floor."

George nodded again. "That's a good idea. Her apartment also has a terrace like ours, and maybe she saw Sunny on the roof. Yes, let's talk to her."

The couple rang the doorbell of their neighbor's apartment, a mixture of anxiety and hope coursing through them. As they waited, they heard a dog barking on the other side of the door. It sounded like a large dog from the tone of its barks. A few minutes passed, and finally, a female voice spoke from behind the door."

The voice sounded sharp and tired, as if it belonged to someone of advanced age. "Who is it?" she asked, looking through the peephole in the door.

Montana spoke up. "Hello, we're your neighbors from the third floor, apartment two."

After a few seconds, the door opened slowly. A musty, stale odor permeated the air, filling it with a sense of ancient moisture. Behind the door stood an older woman; she would be almost eighty years old, of average height, with long, silver hair, somewhat unkempt, and gray, slanted eyes that seemed to contain years of experience. She wore a long green dress with strange golden symbols embroidered on it. Around her neck, she wore a pendant with a round metal medallion with the black figure of what looked like a crow on it.

"Yes, I've seen you come into your apartment on a few occasions," she said with a kind smile, as her voice resonated with a wisdom accumulated over the years. The dog barked again, and the woman immediately reprimanded it. "Shut up, Balor!" exclaimed his owner, and the dog fell silent instantly. It was a relatively small dog despite its loud voice. It was a black Scottish terrier; his right eye seemed different, as if he had some vision problem.

Montana tried to seem friendly as she explained the situation. "He's George, and I'm Montana. Our cat, Sunny, has gone missing, and we thought you might have seen him."

The woman nodded sympathetically. "Oh, that's too bad, poor little animal. My name is Briony; nice to meet you. By the way, how is your cat?"

Montana described Sunny in detail, mentioning his orange fur and inclination to explore rooftops and terraces.

Briony seemed to think for a moment, glancing briefly at her dog Balor, sitting on the floor in a submissive attitude. "I've seen a few cats on the rooftops lately. Balor usually barks to warn me. But none of them match the description of your cat, unfortunately."

Briony frowned as if trying to remember something else as she spoke. "By the way, I remember the former owners of your apartment... they were also young, like you. They lost a cat, a cat that was never seen again."

Montana and George looked at each other, surprised by the unexpected turn of the conversation. "Another missing cat?" Montana asked, with interest and a certain intrigue.

Briony nodded, her wrinkled gray eyes looking back in time. "They had a cat that simply disappeared without a trace. They never knew what happened to him. The poor couple, nothing was the same after their cat disappeared."

George inquired further into the matter, somewhat perplexed by that revelation. "That's curious, isn't it? Two couples are in the same apartment, and both lose their cats. Why do you say nothing was the same?" He asked, very intrigued.

Briony seemed to change her attitude as if mentioning the former tenants brought her gloomy memories. "That couple... they were only here for a few months. It was something tragic."

George's curiosity was growing. "Tragic? What happened?"

Briony sighed. "When their cat disappeared, that young woman was never the same. She was unfortunate and gloomy.

I saw her a few more times, sometimes talking to herself. Until one day, an ambulance came and took her away."

Montana was intrigued. "And the man?"

Briony shook her head. "I never knew what happened to him. He just left the apartment, and I never saw him again. I think the bank ended up with the property, a sad story..." she finished by looking down for a few seconds.

The couple nodded in silence, absorbed by the story. The dark story of their apartment's former owners added a new level of mystery. Briony's dog, Balor, seemed to be showing an expression of curiosity about everything that was being explained there.

Montana felt a chill. "Do you think someone could be behind all this? A neighbor?"

Briony shrugged slightly. "Who knows, dear. Sometimes, evil lurks around, and we don't know where it can come from. But don't worry too much; it doesn't have to happen again. I hope Sunny returns to you soon. If I saw him, I would let you know immediately."

Montana and George were quite worried after hearing those words. They thanked Briony for her attention and said goodbye. As they walked away from the door, the story she told them about the former tenants kept going through their minds, raising more questions about Sunny's disappearance and the mystery surrounding their new home.

CHAPTER 3:

BROKEN INTIMACY

After a sleepless night caused by the wet heat and the uneasiness that the neighbor had instilled in them, the couple woke up with fatigue on their faces. They both went to work. George went to his office that day, designing and printing copies of a poster with the photograph of his missing Sunny to distribute around the neighborhood.

In the afternoon, the scorching summer sun was still felt. The couple began to paste the posters on the streets near their block, on streetlights, and columns and also distributed some posters in mailboxes of the buildings closest to their home.

In the middle of this task, they crossed paths with a woman, probably about eighty or more years old, walking alone in the neighborhood. They showed her Sunny's photo and asked if she had seen the cat.

The older woman, of small stature, with curly hair dyed chestnut, replied that she had seen a similar cat a few hours earlier near her house, but her certainty seemed to waver in her voice. Her doubts aroused suspicions about the older woman's ability to remember things well.

"Thank you, ma'am, for your help," George said gratefully, seeing that they wouldn't get anything out of that woman.

"You're welcome," the woman replied with a smile. Then her expression turned serious. "Be careful, young people. In this neighborhood, as in many places, evil lurks, and not only that, it can also act if it so desires," she warned. At that moment, they saw how she touched a crucifix that she wore around her neck with her trembling fingers.

After the older woman's warning, George and Montana looked at each other, exchanging a few words in thoughtful tones. "Doesn't it seem strange to you that two people in the neighborhood have told us to be careful of evil?" George commented, putting an expression of intrigue on his face.

Montana nodded. "Yes, it does. Briony is her name, right? Our neighbor, the one who told us that disturbing story about the former owners of our apartment, about their cat and how they disappeared in such a dramatic way."

The couple continued their search, approaching people walking their dogs in the park or the neighborhood streets. When they reached the street of the "Orange Buddha's" building, descending from the park down the stainless steel stairs. They followed the street to the east, and George stopped suddenly, contemplating what must have been the entrance to the building of that enigmatic neighbor.

Seeing that the mailboxes were in the lobby and they couldn't quickly enter, he suggested to Montana the idea of affixing one of his posters on one of the columns at the entrance. So they did, hoping that that man or other neighbors, if they had seen Sunny, would decide to contact them.

The days passed, monotonous and without news about Sunny's whereabouts. The concern grew in Montana, who felt deeply affected by losing her beloved pet. Her mood was clouded, and her life took on an apathetic nuance, as if she had lost a part of her being.

One day, George, seeing Montana's mood, decided to take matters into his own hands. He insisted they go out to dinner, trying to get her out of that spiral of sadness. Finally, he convinced her, and they spent a pleasant evening at a good restaurant with a romantic atmosphere. When they returned home, before going to sleep, they made love as they hadn't done in a long time, giving themselves to each other with great passion. This helped them to forget for a moment the last few days of anxiety and accumulated sorrow due to the disappearance of their precious orange feline.

The next day, a few hours after Montana left for work at the store, the figure of the "Orange Buddha" again caught George's attention from the dining room. Driven by an uncontrollable curiosity, he grabbed his digital camera, equipped with a powerful zoom he typically used for bird photography, and headed to his terrace on the upper floor. From there, he had a better view of his enigmatic neighbor without being as quickly seen as he would from the balcony on the lower floor. He aimed the lens at the "Orange Buddha's" room and made out that he was engrossed in writing with a pen, adding a new layer of mystery to his artistic endeavors.

He snapped some photographs of the man in orange and then shifted his attention to the right of the table, where a sheet of paper appeared to contain a new drawing. Focusing his camera there, zooming in to the maximum, and steadying his hand by leaning on the terrace parapet, he managed to discern in detail the content of the drawing placed there. The image that revealed itself left him speechless and entirely surprised. Without wasting any time, George began to capture snapshots of the picture, taking a burst of photographs before it was too late.

The neighbor who smokes cough suddenly rang out. Filled with fear of being discovered while aiming his camera at the door, George quickly crouched behind the parapet of his terrace. He held his breath and waited in silence for a long few seconds. After tension, he gathered his courage and dared to look again towards the neighbor's door, only to find it closed. With his heart still pounding and a mixture of nervousness for what he had witnessed, he reviewed the photographs on the camera screen and decided to continue with his work as best he could.

Hours later, Montana returned from work, hauling the weight of the day's demands. The tension that had momentarily gripped George eased with the presence of his love. However, the uncertainty about Sunny's whereabouts persisted like a constant shadow in their thoughts. With a concerned look, Montana finally broke the silence and asked George if he had any news about her beloved cat.

George replied that there was no news. Montana's sadness was palpable in her eyes as she absorbed the information, resigning herself to the reality that had taken root in their lives. However, George's nervous look made her realize he was hiding something.

Montana asked him, "George, is everything okay? You seem restless. Is something bothering you?"

Feeling guilty for hiding his discovery, George finally gathered the courage to speak. In a hurried and nervous tone, George told Montana he had something important to show her. The seriousness of his expression worried her, and her mind raced through terrifying and hopeful possibilities.

Montana, with a mix of excitement and anxiety, asked what it was about. The worst was going through his mind. Without beating around the bush, George pulled out his camera and cautiously showed the photos he had taken of the drawing to Montana.

In the drawing, one could see a man and a woman having sex; the two naked bodies were drawn with subtle lines, the woman on top of the man and he lying down looking towards her, both in profile.

Montana looked at the photos with a doubtful expression on her face. "It seems this man is quite horny," she commented with a wry smile. He must be a pervert who entertains himself by drawing erotic scenes that he imagines."

George hurried to explain, trying to remain calm. "Doesn't it seem very coincidental to you? We had sex yesterday, and I found this drawing the next day. You wouldn't say that's just a mere coincidence, would you? Besides, he draws a cat and a magpie, and then Sunny disappears, and we see a magpie flying off with his collar..."

Montana interrupted him, cutting him off somewhat impetuously. "George, I understand it seems casual to you, but it's just a drawing. We shouldn't get carried away by absurd theories. Besides, we don't look alike; although the woman has long, light brown hair like me, she has drawn breasts bigger than mine." she commented mockingly to take away some drama from the situation. "And the man in the drawing has short dark brown hair like you, but he has drawn a smaller nose than yours," Montana finished with sarcasm.

George couldn't help but feel that there was something more to all of this, that it wasn't just a coincidence. "Something's fishy here, honey. This can't be just a coincidence. What if that man is spying on us with a hidden camera? It's possible, right?" He began to swiftly search every possible place in the bedroom: walls, furniture, lights...

Montana watched his frantic search with a mixture of concern and dismay. "George, what are you doing? I don't think there's any hidden camera here. This could be a coincidence. That guy must have a hobby for erotic drawings," Montana said, trying to downplay the situation and divert his thoughts from conspiracy theories.

Finally, after carefully checking every corner of the bedroom and finding no sign of a hidden camera, George gave up with a sigh of frustration. Although he still felt something strange about all of this, he decided to give Montana the peace of mind she needed. "Maybe you're right," he admitted, releasing some accumulated tension. "I may be letting my paranoia get the best of me." With a resigned gesture, he collapsed on the bed, trying to dissolve his more surreal thoughts.

CHAPTER 4:

THE ENCOUNTER

The next day, George immersed himself in his work from home again, but the unease persisted, making it hard for him to focus. The revelation of the drawing from that mysterious neighbor, the "Orange Buddha," continued to echo in his mind.

He decided to move to the dining room to observe if that neighbor opened the terrace door or stepped out onto it. After a few hours, he finally saw him come out to smoke a cigarette. George felt it was the moment to address the issue and ask the questions circling his mind. Mustering his courage, he got the man's attention from his balcony.

"Excuse me, sir!" he shouted determinedly, looking at his neighbor. "I want to talk to you. Have you seen our cat? Do you know anything about him?" The neighbor turned his head towards him, a look of indifference behind those round glasses. Without saying a word, he turned around and returned to his room with the cigarette still lit in his mouth, closing the terrace door behind him.

The man's reaction left George surprised and, at the same time, frustrated. That rejection, with barely a word spoken, irked him. Resentment and anger took hold of him, and he couldn't help but shout at him without thinking. "Don't be so rude! What a neighbor!" His voice was filled with frustration and anger in equal measure.

The words echoed in the air, charged with tension and discontent. George felt a mixture of emotions, from rage to concern. He knew that something was wrong with the behavior of that neighbor and was determined to unravel the mystery.

After that failed attempt at conversation, George decided to meet his neighbor face to face. Therefore, he determined to find it when he went out on the street. He began to think about when would be the ideal time. During the following days, he carefully observed his neighbor's routine. He realized that every day around eleven in the morning, he closed the terrace door, turned off the light in his bedroom, and disappeared. A suspicion began to take shape in George's mind: perhaps his neighbor left home as a daily routine then. With this assumption in mind, George decided that the next day, he would wait for him on his street near the exit door at that same time.

The following day, at eleven to four, George left his building, heading to the door of his neighbor's building. In just five minutes, he reached the end of the park and descended the 66 metal steps with stairs separating the park from his neighbor's street. Another five minutes took him near his target; he decided to wait in the doorway of another building, almost opposite where his neighbor lived. Luckily, he didn't get the sun, as the day was very sunny and hot. He waited patiently. Some people passed by walking and looked at him briefly with curious faces, but George didn't care; he was determined to be able to talk face-to-face with his rude neighbor.

George looked at his watch; it was eleven o'clock in the morning, and so far, nothing, but after a few minutes, he detected movement in the lobby of his neighbor's building. His heart beat a little faster when he glimpsed the figure of the man dressed in his distinctive orange t-shirt and beige shorts. There was no doubt it was his neighbor. With his pulse racing, George started moving towards him. Upon noticing his presence, the man began to increase the pace of his steps in the direction of the stairs that led up to the park. The tension in the air was palpable as George approached.

The man walked at a surprisingly fast pace despite his corpulence. George realized he could not catch him walking and decided to get his attention: "Excuse me, sir," he shouted, his voice echoing in the street. "I'm your neighbor in front of your terrace; I want to talk to you briefly." However, the orange man did not even bother to turn his head and increased his pace even more.

George hoped that once the man reached the stairs, he would have the opportunity to catch him on the ascent. But to his amazement, he watched the neighbor climb the stairs with unusual speed, even though the man was overweight.

The scene was quite surreal. The neighbor climbed the stairs with unexpected agility, almost feline, and George chased him, driven by the need for answers. The distance between them gradually decreased, and as George's heart pounded with the effort of climbing so quickly, he knew he was about to have a face-to-face encounter with that mysterious neighbor.

When he reached the top of the stairs, George considered the possibility of starting to run to catch him and thus force a conversation. Just as he was about to do so, a sharp caw rang out to his right. Instinctively, he looked over there and saw a magpie perched on a branch of a nearby tree; his heart raced even faster.

Surprised and confused, George returned to where he had seen the fugitive, only to discover that he had disappeared. He ran a few yards in the direction he assumed the orange man had taken but found no trace of him. He looked back and saw that the magpie had also disappeared.

Frustrated by the futile chase and with his heart pounding, George decided to return to the fugitive neighbor's building. He positioned himself on the same street where he had waited for him, observing patiently. However, as time passed and the neighbor failed to arrive, George attempted to enter the building. He rang the doorbells of the residents, posing as a gas company representative. Eventually, someone unlocked the electric door.

Once inside the building, he sought out the mailboxes and located the ones on the fifth floor. "John Lugh," he murmured, convinced this must be the mailbox of the elusive "Orange Buddha," as the other one bore a woman's name. While he waited, a building resident entered from the street and spotted him in the lobby. She inquired if he was expecting someone, and George informed her he was waiting for John Lugh, the neighbor on the fifth floor. The neighbor regarded him with suspicion and retorted curtly, "I wasn't aware my neighbor had any friends."

The woman proceeded to the elevator without saying another word. She wore a stern expression and cast a wary glance toward George as she summoned the elevator and stepped inside. Since a few minutes had passed without the "Orange Buddha" appearing, George chose to head back to his apartment to avoid any potentially awkward encounters with other residents. With each step he took toward his home, his intrigue and bewilderment deepened as he pondered the mysteries that enigmatic neighbor named John Lugh might be concealing.

CHAPTER 5:

BENEATH THE SURFACE OF APPEARANCES

George arrived at his apartment feeling uneasy. He needed answers and didn't want to be left hanging. He sat in front of his laptop, started to investigate, and typed the name "John Lugh" into several internet browsers, hoping to find some trace that would lead him to understand who his neighbor really was.

The search results were varied, but unfortunately, no data matched his neighbor. No social media profiles checked his neighbor, not even about his hobby of drawing or writing. He also found no clues by adding the town's name where they lived. The lack of results only increased the mystery surrounding John Lugh.

However, he did discover something. He realized that "Lugh" was a name of Celtic origin. He also found that "Lugh" was the name of the Celtic god of the sun, light, war, and harvest and was associated with art and craftsmanship.

Suddenly, a memory came to his mind. He remembered his neighbor Briony, the woman in the green dress adorned with those peculiar golden symbols with a Celtic look. A strange idea began to take shape in his mind: What if Briony, by chance, knew more about that voyeuristic neighbor named John Lugh? The possibility of getting answers prompted him to talk to his neighbor again.

With the decision made, George headed for Briony's door. As he was about to ring the doorbell, he heard a familiar sound: the barking of that small Scottish terrier. But this time, he listened to a sharp "tssssit" behind the door that silenced the dog. He felt like he was being watched through the peephole in the door. After a few seconds, the door slowly opened, and Briony appeared. Once again, he perceived that musty smell, like ancient moisture, emanating from the older woman's apartment.

Their eyes met, and George could perceive a mixture of surprise and curiosity in the older woman's gaze. "Oh, It's you again, my neighbor down the hall!" she exclaimed with a smile. The older woman's voice was sweet and drawn out, tinged with curiosity. "What do you want, if I may ask?" she continued, looking at him expectantly.

George started by apologizing, "Excuse me if I bother you. I would like to ask again if you have seen our cat, Sunny."

The old woman replied: "Unfortunately, I haven't seen any cats roaming around my terrace for a few days. Even Balor, my dog, hasn't noticed the presence of any cats on the roofs or our terrace."

With a friendly expression, George took the opportunity to continue the conversation. He asked Briony if she knew anything about a neighbor who lived in the six-story building down the street, to the south, and who always wore an orange t-shirt. He also described him to her, hoping to find clues about the enigmatic "Orange Buddha." Briony furrowed her brow slightly and took a moment to think.

"I don't remember seeing anyone like that in the neighborhood," Briony finally replied; the woman seemed a little frustrated. George, not losing hope, decided to dig a little deeper. "Maybe the name John Lugh sounds familiar to you," he hinted cautiously.

When the older woman heard that name, George noticed her expression change, becoming more severe and harsh. She spoke slowly, "No, I don't know that name. It doesn't ring me a bell."

Although Briony denied knowing the name, George didn't quite believe her answer. There was a change in Briony's attitude that didn't go unnoticed by him.

The conversation continued, and Briony added, "Young man, remember what I told you when we first met about how evil lurks, and we never know where it may come from? It wouldn't be absurd to think this John Lugh has something to do with your cat's disappearance. He could have been watching you from his apartment on the other side of the courtyards. As I told you, the cat of the previous owners of your apartment also disappeared."

George felt disturbed, considering the possibility that the older woman had been aware of his enigmatic neighbor and had not told them anything clearly when they came to her for the first time.

At that moment, Briony took out of a pocket what looked like a pendant in her dress. "I'm going to give you a gift," she said solemnly. "Please don't refuse it. It means a lot to me.

It's a Celtic amulet, a triquetra. It protects the wearer from the forces of evil."

George was stunned by the older woman's gesture but extended his hand to receive the pendant out of courtesy. "Thank you," he replied, somewhat overwhelmed. "Although I don't believe in superstitions," he took the bright metal amulet and looked at it briefly, seeing that it had a triangular shape composed of three intertwined arches. He remembered seeing something like it on the internet or in a cheap jewelry store.

Briony said goodbye with a wise look in her eyes. "I hope it protects you from the evil that lurks around us in this eternal struggle between good and evil. Because beneath the surface of appearances, one can find the very evil. Evil is much older than the human species; it existed long before the first man began to walk upright. Until soon, young man. Take good care of your beautiful wife, and may you be lucky."

George was undoubtedly uneasy after hearing all that. And it came to his mind that octogenarian neighbor they met in the street clutching that small crucifix in her fingers. Not knowing what to say, he stammered a "Goodbye, ma'am," as she retired, closing the door before George's astonished gaze. She left him with even more questions and a sense of unease.

As he returned to his apartment, the conversation with Briony resonated in his mind. He felt the metal of the amulet in his hand, warmed by the skin that enveloped it, and although he did not believe in all those stories of good versus evil that the older woman had tried to instill in him, he could not help but feel a momentary chill running down his back. After a few hours, Montana's arrival comforted him, and he decided to share with her everything that had happened to him that day, such intense emotions.

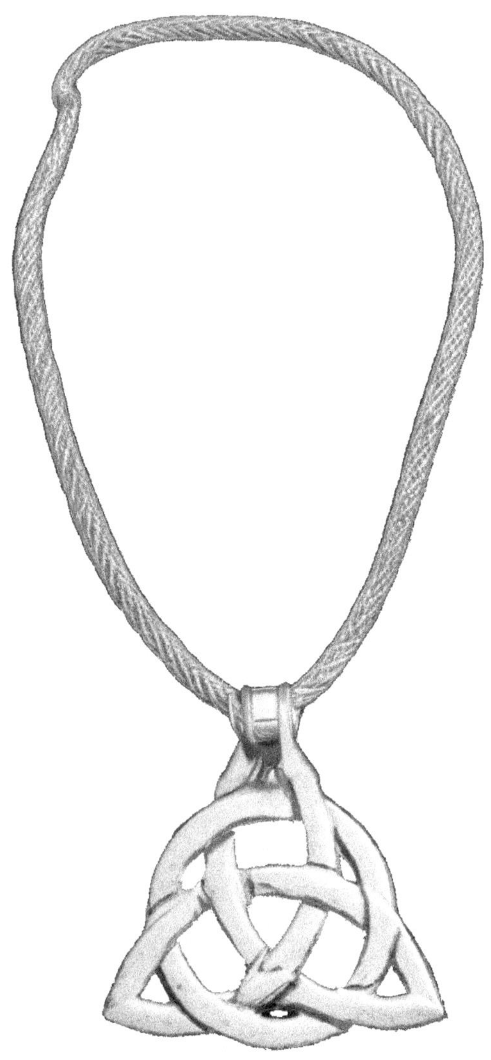

CHAPTER 6:

THE AMULET

"I can't believe it, George," Montana exclaimed in amazement. "Did you really go to meet that man? To wait for him outside his house? You know he could call the police and accuse you of harassment. What a shame, George! Don't you think you've gone too far?"

George responded with a mixture of determination and frustration. "Honey, I needed to do something. I tried talking to him from the balcony days ago, and he ignored me like I didn't exist. And what about the magpie appearing to me in the park? I can't help but feel that there's something more going on that we can't see. And, honestly, doesn't it seem strange that someone with so much overweight can climb the stairs so quickly? That neighbor is not what he seems."

Montana reflected on George's words, trying to understand the situation. "Well, the fact that he climbed the stairs so quickly could have a logical explanation. Maybe he's in much better physical condition than he appears. And, as for the magpie, it could just be a coincidence, don't you think?

Always is seen some magpies in the park. When I think about what could have happened to Sunny, I get unfortunate. Will he be with someone? Or has something bad happened to him?"

But George didn't give up and continued, "Yes, but don't forget that, as an amateur ornithologist, I know very well that magpies almost always travel in pairs, and this one was alone. It's possible that it was the same individual we saw with Sunny's collar."

Montana replied, "Yes, George, I know you know about birds, but as you said, they almost always travel in pairs, not always."

George continued to be obsessed, "But wait, there's something more disturbing: that man's name is John Lugh; I could see it in his mailbox. After researching, I discovered that his last name, Lugh, coincides with the name of a Celtic god associated with the sun, war, and art. In addition, I went to talk to Briony about him, since I remembered that she was wearing that green dress with those symbols that looked Celtic. Do you remember? I thought she might know something more about that last name."

Montana looked at him with vehemence. "Lugh must be a surname of Irish origin and nothing more. Surely, there are hundreds of people if you search the internet with this last name. But, wait a minute, did you talk to our neighbor about all this?"

George nodded with a mixture of nervousness and shame. "Yes, I asked her if she knew anything about Sunny, and then I took the opportunity to mention that neighbor's name. Her expression changed radically when I said it and became earnest. She started talking again about the evil that lurked around us and suggested that this man could be related to Sunny's disappearance. She even hinted that he's been watching us."

Suddenly, George showed her the Celtic amulet that Briony had given him, holding it in the air by the cord. "Look at this, Montana. She gave me this metal amulet. A triquetra, she told me it's called. According to her, it's used to protect oneself from evil."

Montana looked at the amulet skeptically. "George, all of this sounds a bit like superstition. Do you really believe this metal piece can protect you from anything? Honestly, the amulet looks more like a trinket. I've seen similar pendants in cheap jewelry stores or flea market stalls."

George responded calmly, "Yes, I thought the same thing about the amulet when Briony gave it to me. But wait a moment!" he exclaimed, very agitated, "I think I've seen something similar somewhere else recently." Without wasting time, he rushed to grab his camera and began reviewing his photos of the neighbor writing in his room just before photographing that erotic drawing. He found three pictures of the neighbor in front of his desk, and he could see that he was wearing a metal pendant around his neck. George zoomed in on the best of the three images in the chest area, and with attentive eyes, he observed that it was some kind of amulet. Without wasting time, he hurried to show the enlarged image to Montana.

She observed the image with astonishment, her eyes fixed on the amulet the man wore on his chest. "It's true! I must admit that it does seem to have something in common with Briony's amulet; it looks like three intertwined spirals. But, what could all this mean?"

George shrugged, sharing the same bewilderment. "I don't know, Montana. Let's search on the internet for what we can find."

George went to get his laptop and turned it on. After typing the two keywords "Celtic amulets" into a search engine, a results list appeared. To his surprise, the first one on the list looked very similar to the one the neighbor was wearing: a triskelion.

Montana was stunned by the discovery. George read aloud: "The triskelion is a symbol of three spirals joined together that represent the trinity. It is also associated with power and strength. It is said that the triskelion protects its wearer from the forces of evil."

Montana commented in surprise, "Look, another Celtic amulet for protection from evil. And what about the one Briony gave you? Does it appear here?"

After a few seconds, George continued browsing the website and found other information. "Here it is, the triquetra," he said as he read aloud: "The triquetra is a symbol of three curves joined together that represent the past, the present, and the future. It is also associated with the trinity, fertility, and eternity. It is said that the triquetra protects its wearer from the forces of evil."

The room filled with an uneasy silence as George and Montana absorbed the information. The connection between the two amulets, the "Orange Buddha" amulet, and their elderly neighbor's seemed too much of a coincidence. The older woman's allusions to the fact that evil can be found in the most unexpected places beneath the surface of appearances.

George finally said, aware that it all sounded crazy, "I know, Montana. It sounds far-fetched. But something about this whole story makes me think there is a connection between that man and the old woman, and I'll tell you more: with Sunny's disappearance, and it could even be that with the tragic end of the couple who lived here."

With the night advancing and all those speculations running through his mind, George was determined to unravel the mystery surrounding that man, "John Lugh." Even though it might be dangerous, even though he might be going too far, he couldn't ignore the feeling that a dark and bewildering force was lurking around them.

CHAPTER 7:

EVIL RISES TO THE SURFACE

The next day, George decided to stay home and work on his laptop while Montana left for the store. They briefly kissed goodbye, and she said, "Goodbye, honey, have a good day." He replied, "You too, my love."

George was still utterly obsessed with his neighbor. He stared at the man's terrace. Although he could see light inside the room, the neighbor's terrace door remained closed; there was no sign of the man in orange.

A few hours passed, and a storm moved in from the north. Thunders could be heard getting closer. Thick drops of rain began to fall from the sky; within minutes, it was pouring.

George went to the balcony, and looking through the curtain of rain, his gaze fell almost instinctively to the door of the "Orange Buddha." To his surprise, he saw a piece of orange paper stuck to the glass from the inside. He ran to get his binoculars and, focusing on the paper through the slightly fogged glass, he could make out a word written in capital letters, in thick red ink on the orange paper: "COME."

He couldn't believe what he was seeing. A whirlwind of contradictory thoughts crossed his mind: from the possibility that the man finally wanted to be honest with him to the doubt that it could be a sinister trap. However, he decided to muster his courage, looked out again, and noticed that the rain was stopping. He took the amulet that Briony had given him from his desk, almost without thinking, perhaps hoping it might somehow be helpful to him, and put it in the pocket of his short-sleeved polo shirt in a deep turquoise blue.

As he descended the stairs to the exit of the building, the barking of Balor, Briony's terrier, could be heard from the older woman's apartment. He reached the street and immediately headed towards the park; it was still drizzling, and thunders rumbled in the distance. He descended with some caution down the wet steel stairs, reaching the beginning of the neighbor's street.

In a few minutes, George was at the door of the "Orange Buddha's" building. He tried to push it to open, discovering that it was unlocked. Someone had released the electric bolt from some floor before his arrival; he thought it was probably that strange neighbor. Then, even though a shiver ran down his body from head to toe, he decided to continue with some caution. He called the elevator to come down but immediately reflected on the advisability of riding it. Finally, he chose to be distrustful and climb the stairs from the ground floor to the fifth floor, even though it would be a bit of a workout.

When he reached the landing on the fifth floor, he noticed that the door to the fifth-floor apartment was ajar. His heart was pounding, but he faced his fears and moved forward. He pushed the door open cautiously and called, "Hello? Is anyone there?" He noticed a strong scent of moss, similar to the fragrance that evokes an ancient forest. He experienced a strange sensation upon finding this scent in that place.

A warm light filtered in from the end of the hallway, and George approached it step by step. "Hey, Mr. Lugh, are you there?" he shouted. Then he continued, "What do you want from us? Why are you doing this?"

When he reached the door to the room, he saw that no one was inside. He entered, and his gaze immediately fell on the table; the man had made a new drawing. The image chilled his blood: a woman with long hair lay on the floor, surrounded by a large pool of blood. Above her, he had drawn a rainbow. George was stunned to see that macabre drawing. Underneath the woman's body, he could read: "Briony Morrigan," written in cursive. Could that be the full name of his neighbor? Something told him it might well be.

He saw some sheets of paper scattered on the table, with strange symbols that the man had probably written for hours. He detected a repetitive pattern in their content as if he were repeating the exact phrases repeatedly, as if it were a mantra. A sudden noise from the entrance made him turn abruptly, catching a glimpse of a figure disappearing through the apartment door; there was no doubt that it was the one with the "Orange Buddha". He then heard how he began to descend the stairs in a hurry. Without thinking, he followed him in his escape.

George ran out onto the landing of the stairs, shouted, "Wait, don't run!" and, without thinking, pressed the button to call the elevator to reach him on the ground floor. The elevator ascended slowly; the door opened, he jumped in and pressed the button for the ground floor. The door closed and began to descend gradually. It braked abruptly, and the door opened, revealing the lobby. George rushed out of the elevator just in time to see the orange man in the hall, leaving for the street at a fantastic speed. He started running after him, seeing that the man was going to the right, towards the park's stairs. When George reached the street, he stopped short. He looked to the right but couldn't see anyone. Then he looked to the left, and still, no one. The fugitive had utterly disappeared. He couldn't believe what was happening; he thought, "How can that man have completely disappeared? I came out just seconds after him to the street."

Baffled, he returned to his building as soon as possible, quickly climbing the stairs to the park, considering the possibility that that neighbor was deliberately playing with him. When he reached his entrance, he thought of something: looking at the mailboxes. He went over to them and checked his neighbor's name on the landing; it was written: "Mrs. Morrigan and Balor." His neighbor Briony was named Briony Morrigan, the same name he had seen in the terrible drawing in that neighbor's house.

A jumble of thoughts and theories flooded his mind; none seemed to make sense. What was the relationship between Briony Morrigan and that man named John Lugh? Why had he made that disturbing drawing with his neighbor's name at the bottom? How could that corpulent man have vanished into thin air? George felt trapped in an enigma that was becoming increasingly intricate and dark.

CHAPTER 8:

EVIL EMERGES FROM THE SURFACE

George went to his apartment and noticed that Montana had arrived home. Seeing that she had left her purse on the coat rack and feeling a draft, he called out to her: "Honey, where are you?"

Getting no answer, he climbed the wooden steps to the upper floor of the duplex, noticing that the sliding French window of the terrace was open, and called out again: "Honey, are you out there?"

Amid his confusion, he heard Montana's voice shouting, "George, I'm here on the roof of the building next door! I've seen Sunny!"

George hurriedly went to the terrace and looked to his right, where the shouts came from. He saw Montana walking across the roof, still wet from the rain, half-crouched near the edge. "George, Sunny was here. I have seen him! Sunny, come here to mama!"

Worried, George shouted: "Montana, come back! I don't see Sunny, this is dangerous!"

Montana turned to him again, and at that moment, her left foot slipped, and she lost her balance. She fell to the roof and rolled towards the edge, plunging into the void. A heart-wrenching scream from Montana echoed in the air, followed by the jarring sound of her body hitting the ground.

George quickly approached the edge of the terrace and looked down, his heart pounding in his chest.

He saw below, on a terrace on the ground floor, Montana's body on the ground, motionless, a pool of blood slowly spreading. He stood frozen, unable to believe what he saw, and cried out in despair: "No!" putting his hands on his head.

Immediately, he heard a scream coming from the terrace where Montana's body had fallen. George saw a woman looking up at him from below; their eyes met briefly in an anguish-filled silence. With tears in his eyes and his hands on his head, George kneeled, hiding behind the terrace wall, talking to himself: "This can't be, this can't be real."

A few seconds passed, which felt like an eternity, with tears in his eyes for the immense tragedy he had just witnessed. Finally, he got up and, with his gaze almost lost downwards, saw the "Orange Buddha" on his terrace, impassively observing what had happened. George exchanged a look full of hatred with that man; the latter showed not a hint of surprise at the fatal fall.

The neighbor turned around and returned to his room, closing the door behind him. George could not believe that attitude, so cold and lacking in empathy. At that very moment, the storm, which had witnessed the tragedy, gave way to a distant rainbow in the sky.

A sharp pain pierced his temples, and a wave of rage grew inside him, directed towards that man in orange, who seemed to have foreshadowed in his drawing and perhaps desired the tragedy that had just occurred. George walked determinedly to the kitchen and grabbed the most giant knife he could find.

Without closing the door behind him, he hurriedly left his apartment and descended the stairs quickly. In the entrance hall, he met a neighbor of the building who looked at him with amazement and concern when he saw him wielding the vast knife with an expression of anger.

George ran out into the street and quickly headed towards the park. A couple walking by was stunned to see him with the knife. The emergency services sirens began to sound in the distance, alerted by the neighbor of the terrace where Montana's body lay.

He reached the steel stairs and descended hastily down the metal steps. On the last landing, when he was only a dozen steps from the bottom of the stairs, he heard a squawk nearby to his right. Startled, he turned sharply to look, but the metal staircase was slippery from the rain, and he lost his balance.

He plummeted down the metal steps, dropping the knife. The metallic sound of the knife hitting the steps echoed as George rolled down the stairs, unable to stop himself. Finally, he reached the ground of the sidewalk and stopped, lying unconscious on the cold and wet pavement of the sidewalk.

In his mind, a carousel of images paraded: Montana on the floor of the terrace, the blood spreading, the icy gaze of the "Orange Buddha," the sinister drawing in the room, the hand of his neighbor Briony holding the amulet, the pictures of his cat Sunny and the magpie, the magpie with the collar of his pet.

While he lay on the ground, the magpie landed near him. It took a few graceful hops on the ground and picked up the pendant with its beak; the amulet had come out of George's polo pocket in the fall. After taking the pendant, it took flight, climbing the stairs until it landed on a tree in the park.

After a few minutes, George slowly regained consciousness, although he felt dizzy from the harsh fall. He soon started to notice the scent of dampness in the air. Looking up, he saw a man dressed in his blue uniform and police cap. The agent's words sounded like a distant echo in his head: "Sir, don't move. The ambulance will be here soon."

In the distance, a female voice began to speak on the radio: "Central, this is unit 605. We have a possible 10-53. We found the suspect on the ground, at the foot of the stairs in the northwest park. He is conscious but appears to have suffered a concussion due to a fall. We need medical assistance to assess his condition. We found the knife with which he was seen on the ground near him. Please notify the homicide squad."

From the central, a male voice responded, preceded by a brief beep on the radio: "Unit 605, received. We confirm the report of a possible 10-53. The victim appears to be a woman found in a nearby building, where unit 609 and medical services have been dispatched. We have alerted the homicide squad to proceed to their positions. Remain on the scene until they arrive. Unit 602 is headed to your position to guard the suspect if it is necessary to transfer him to the hospital."

The magpie, amid the din of sirens and flashing strobe lights from emergency vehicles, took flight from its perch carrying the Celtic pendant in its beak. It descended gracefully and landed on the wall of a nearby terrace. With a deliberate movement, it left the metal amulet on the gray stone that crowned the wall and emitted a new squawk.

A few seconds passed, and the sliding French window leading to the terrace opened, revealing the frail figure of an older woman. It was Briony Morrigan, with her green dress billowing in the wind and her silver hair disheveled;

she slowly walked towards where the magpie was perched. Suddenly, with its contrasting colors, black and white like yin and yang, the magpie took flight, emitting a new squawk as if it were saying goodbye to the older woman.

Briony picked up the metal amulet with a thoughtful expression and looked at it for a few moments. Then, with serenity, she put it in the pocket of her dress, where the Celtic symbols embroidered in gold seemed to come to life under the light of dusk.

Her gray eyes were lost in thought as if she were visualizing the tragedy that had just happened. It was as if what had happened had nothing to do with her when it was quite the opposite. Evil was part of her essence, an uncontrollable force that drove her to act. To act in this world, which had changed so much, too much, to her regret.

So many centuries had passed since her appearance. She was born thanks to the imagination of the men and women who created her, her, and so many other mythological beings. Made up of the brightest and most miserable of humanity. With good and evil as the primary colors of a palette with endless shades.

Perhaps the longing for those glorious ancestral times, before she had almost completely fallen into the oblivion of men, drove her to act against those who did not deserve it? Or was it the envy aroused by seeing the love between that young couple? Who could know what was going through the mind of the Celtic goddess Morrigan? With a look full of nostalgia fixed on the sunset, her thoughts faded into the twilight of that warm summer day.

Morrigan is the goddess of life and death, of love and war. She is the force of nature, the energy that shapes the world.

Balor, son of the god Lugh, leader of the Fomorii giants, lord of death, the bringer of destruction.

CELTIC MYTHOLOGY

Dear reader,

Thank you for reaching the end of my book. If you enjoyed it, would you consider leaving a review on Amazon or other platforms and recommending it to other readers?

As I mentioned in the prologue, your feedback is crucial in helping me continue to create more stories like this.

I appreciate your time and support in advance.

J. F. Rhodehouse